READY, SET, SCHOOL!

By **Jacquelyn Mitchard**

Illustrated by **Paul Rátz de Tagyos**

HarperCollins Publishers

Manufactured in China. All rights reserved.
No part of this book may be used or reproduced in any manner whatsoever without
written permission except in the case of brief quotations embodied in critical
articles and reviews. For information address HarperCollins Children's Books,
a division of HarperCollins Publishers, 1350 Avenue of the Americas, New York, NY 10019.
www.harpercollinschildrens.com

Library of Congress Cataloging-in-Publication Data is available.
ISBN-10: 0-06-050766-7 (trade bdg.) — ISBN-13: 978-0-06-050766-4 (trade bdg.)
ISBN-10: 0-06-050767-5 (lib. bdg.) — ISBN-13: 978-0-06-050767-1 (lib. bdg.)

Typography by Carla Weise
1 2 3 4 5 6 7 8 9 10
❖
First Edition

For Atticus
—J.M.

Deep inside his trout-shaped sleeping bag,
Rory was hiding from his parents.

"Rory!" his mama and papa called, as they
searched every crevice in their hollow-tree
home to find him. "Hey, little bandit! Time
to go to Aunt Ramona's house!"

Rory didn't move a whisker, even when he heard his papa clambering up the branches to Rory's room.

"Rory!" Papa called. "I know you're up there somewhere! You'll miss the apple and sardine pie your aunt is making just for you! The moon's coming up! Your cousins are going to go play in the dark without you!"

As you know, raccoons stay awake all night. During the dark they work and play.

But Rory just crossed his paws and snuggled down deeper into his sleeping bag. His favorite goldfish pajamas were packed inside, along with his *Rocket Raccoon* comic book. Everything was ready for Rory's sleepover—except Rory!

Just then, he heard a soft voice say, "I see a little round lump in that sleeping bag. Rory, my trout pal, come on out." That was Mama.

"We're going to be late," said another voice. *That* was Papa.

Twice a year at midnight, Rory's parents went out to a gourmet garbage party. They'd tip over all the trash cans behind the fanciest houses! It was a dressy event, and all the raccoons spent days getting their fur done and their claws buffed. Usually Grandma Rebecca stayed with Rory. But tonight she was going with his parents, and Rory had to stay over at his aunt Ramona's house.

When he first heard about his sleepover, Rory was excited about staying with his twin cousins, Roy and Ray. Then he remembered! It would be his first day away from home!

Rory knew he wasn't a baby kit anymore. He just *couldn't* admit he didn't want to go! Still, he didn't feel happy when his parents weren't nearby. And yet in just one week, he would be starting school at Remarkable Raccoon Suburban School. He would learn all sorts of new things, such as garage-door safety and how to tell if round, red things were balloons or pieces of fruit.

He would learn how to open garden gates with his paws and bury food in cold places. He would learn stories and songs. He'd have to walk across the big field with Ralph and Rita, his friends who lived on the golf course, and take his lunch in his Rocket Raccoon backpack.

He'd be at school every night almost until morning! He had to be ready. And staying over at Aunt Ramona's was the best way to practice.

Rory did worry about being at school all night, but he worried more about being away from home. That was why he finally decided to hide.

When he did come out at last, Mama and Papa asked, "Ready, set, go?"

Rory yelled,

 "NO!"

"Why not, bandit?" Papa asked.

Rory said, "I changed my mind! Anyhow, why do you have to go? Don't you love me more than some dumb garbage party? Can't I come too?" His parents shook their heads again, and smiled.

"Rory," Mama said, "there's no one we love more than you. But gourmet garbage parties aren't for kits. And you wouldn't want to disappoint your cousins. They are expecting you. Raccoons live in families and depend on one another. It's not as if we were . . . cats or something!"

Papa added then, "You *do* love your aunt and uncle, and your cousins have the biggest dead tree in the woods! Twenty whole branches! And know what? I'll bet they'll let you stay up until the sun rises!"

"Well, I hope they don't stay up *too* late in the morning," Mama said. "Ray and Roy are forest kits. They're a little wild. Ramona lets them hang from branches by their feet. . . ."

Hang by their feet? Well, suddenly things didn't sound so bad!

Rory started to roll up his sleeping bag. He followed his
mama and papa down the branches. But as soon as his paws
touched the ground, big fat tears started rolling down his
cheeks.

His papa and mama rushed to hug him.

"Maybe he has a tummy ache," Papa said to Mama. "That watermelon rind he had for dinner didn't look very rotten to me."

"It was practically squishy!" Mama said. "Just right for a growing boy! I wouldn't give my little kit anything that would hurt him."

"I don't have a tummy ache," Rory yelled, "and I'm not a little kit! I just don't like new places! I'm not going. So there!"

"What's really bothering you, Rory?" Mama asked.

"Well, really, it's that you might never come back," Rory admitted. "Garbage parties aren't safe for parents either."

Papa nodded. "My folks went to gourmet garbage night when I was a kit, and I used to get scared of that same thing. Every time my folks tried to take me to Grandpa Randall's, I'd kick up a fuss. But when I finally went, I had so much fun fishing that I couldn't wait to go back. New things can be scary, but when you try them, most of the time they're fun!"

Rory thought that over. If Papa could do it, well, he could, too! So off the family went, down the driveways and across the golf course and into the woods.

And, surprise,

he had a great time!

Rory and his cousins caught minnows and slid in the mud.
They hung by their toes and stayed up way past daylight.
Rory didn't forget his parents, but he never felt like crying to
go home. He had barely settled down in his sleeping bag when
his mom and dad picked him up, right on time.

Papa carried him home, and he woke feeling fine. His parents brought him two big cookies, missing only one bite, and an old rubber boot to keep his bottle cap collection in.

But the best part was that Rory didn't feel like a fraidy kit anymore.

He started counting the days until school.

When the morning before school finally came, Rory packed all his school supplies in his Rocket Raccoon backpack. He packed brand-new sticks for prying open cans, a water bottle, and something special for show and share. He chose his broken cat collar with the five bells. Before bed, he helped Mama make his lunch.

"Now, Rory," Mama said, "don't forget to wash your paws. And rinse your apple cores and broken eggs three times. Be careful not to get your prying sticks near your eyes."

That night, Rory's friends Ralph and Rita came to pick him up at his tree.

But his parents wanted to walk with them across the golf course! "We're not really going *with* you," Mama explained. "We just saw some old paper plates with ketchup on them over by the clubhouse that we wanted to rip up."

"Okay," Rory said. "Ready, set, go?"

But Mama and Papa yelled, "NO!"

"You can go to school next year, when you're bigger," Mama said.

"It might be best to stay home a little longer," Papa said.

Rory gave them a big hug and stepped away. "Papa and Mama, you know I have to learn all the things you learned at school, fishing and scratching and tipping trash cans and everything! After all, I'm not a little kit anymore."

Rory's parents nodded bravely. But when he turned to wave one last time, Papa started to sniffle and Mama had a tear in her eye.

"Golly, don't cry!" Rory said. "Most new things are scary, right, Papa? You just have to give them a try. It will all be fine, you'll see! And don't worry—I won't be late, just like you weren't late when you went out. I think I'll like school, but home will still be my favorite place."

Papa said, "I think our Rory is ready to go."

Mama said, "You're sure you're all set?"

And Rory took a deep breath and said,
"YES!"